under The sea

Sue Mayfield ✳ Illustrated by Sue Hendra

EGMONT
We bring stories to life

Book Band: Green

First published in Great Britain 2012
by Egmont UK Ltd
239 Kensington High Street, London W8 6SA
Text copyright © Sue Mayfield 2012
Illustrations copyright © Sue Hendra 2012
The author and illustrator have asserted their moral rights.
ISBN 978 1 4052 5676 6
10 9 8 7 6 5 4 3 2 1
A CIP catalogue record for this title is available from the British Library.
Printed in Singapore.
48094/1

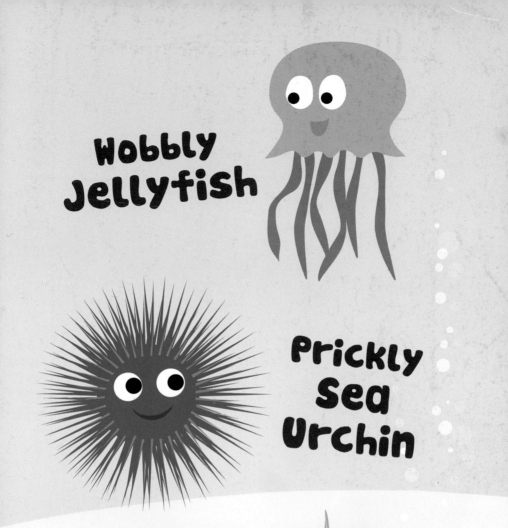

Wobbly
Jellyfish

Prickly
Sea
Urchin

Fabulous
Fish

To Sylvie
S. M.

For Yasmine
S. H.

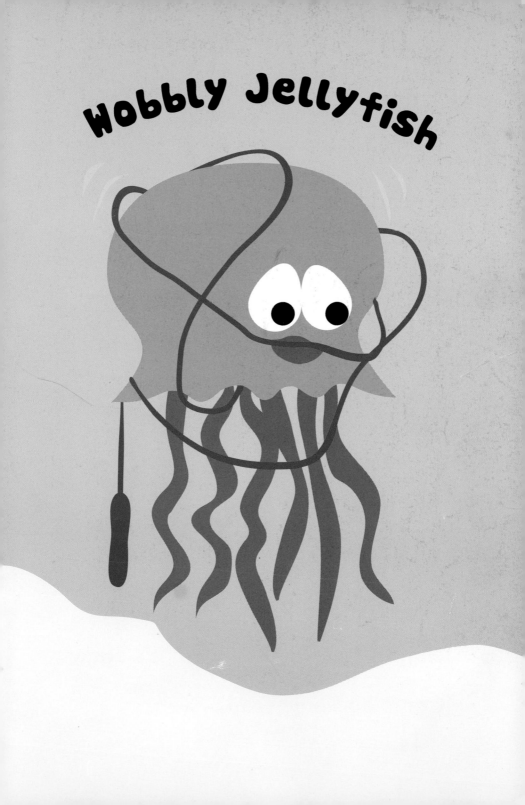

Wobbly Jellyfish

Jellyfish isn't very brave.

Sometimes she gets wobbly.

It's too dark!

Jellyfish gets wobbly when it's dark.

'Come and hide,' says Crab.

Jellyfish gets wobbly when the water is cold.

'Come and swim,' says Angel Fish.

It's too cold!

Jellyfish gets wobbly when friends
ask her to play.

'Come and skip,' says Seahorse.

'I'm too shy,' says Jellyfish.

'Don't be wobbly,' says Angel Fish.

'It's silly to be wobbly,' says Seahorse.

'I WISH I wasn't wobbly,' says

Jellyfish.

Oh dear.

Then one day there is a new girl at school.

'This is Octopus,' says Teacher. 'I need someone to look after her.'

Hello!

'Choose me!' says Angel Fish.

'Choose me!' says Crab.

'Choose me!' says Seahorse.

'I choose Jellyfish,' says the teacher.

'But SHE'S TOO WOBBLY!'

everyone says.

Jellyfish shows Octopus where to put
her coat.

She shows Octopus where to eat her lunch.

She shows Octopus where to go to the toilet!

At playtime they swim down deep.

The water isn't cold at all.

They play hide and seek.

The dark is fun.

Hee hee!

Jellyfish teaches Octopus to skip and when Octopus gets tangled up Jellyfish laughs.

When Dad comes, Jellyfish says,
'I made a new friend, and I wasn't
wobbly ALL day.'

Dad gives Jellyfish a big hug.

'Well done!' he says.

Prickly Sea Urchin

Sea Urchin is very prickly.

He is covered all over with sharp,

sharp prickles.

When Sea Urchin plays with the other fish his prickles get in the way.

Sea Urchin plays hide and seek with
Starfish.

But Starfish says, 'Ouch! Your
prickles hurt!'

Sea Urchin plays hopscotch with Octopus.

But Octopus says, 'Mind out! Your prickles are sharp!'

Sea Urchin plays catch with Seahorse.

But Seahorse says, 'Oh no! Your prickles have popped the ball.'

Sorry!

24

Nobody wants to play with Sea Urchin.

'You're too prickly!' everyone says.

Sea Urchin is sad. He sits under a rock and watches the other fish play.

He watches Angel Fish play hide
and seek with Seahorse.

He watches Octopus play hopscotch
with Jellyfish.

He watches Starfish play catch with Crab.

'I wish I wasn't prickly,' Sea Urchin says.

Then one day a new friend comes along. The new friend looks just like Sea Urchin.

The new friend is covered in sharp, sharp prickles.

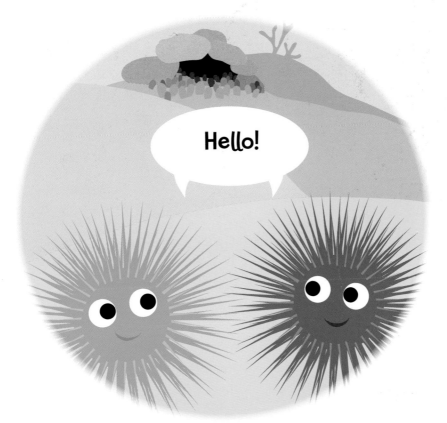

'You're just like me,' Sea Urchin says. 'You're all prickly!'

'Let's play!' says Sea Urchin's new friend.

So the two sea urchins play. They play hide and seek. They play hopscotch.

And when they play catch and the
ball pops on their prickles . . .
they laugh and laugh and laugh.

Ha ha ha!

Fabulous Fish is fabulous in every way.

Fabulous Fish has fabulous stripes.

Fabulous Fish has fabulous fins.

Fabulous Fish has a fabulous tail.

'Look at me!' says Fabulous Fish.

'I'm fabulous!'

Fabulous Fish is good at everything.

Fabulous Fish can swim very fast.

Fabulous Fish can twirl and spin.

Wheee!

Fabulous Fish can even play the

violin.

Oh my!

'Look at me!' says Fabulous Fish.

'I'm fabulous!'

Crab likes to paint.

'My painting is better,' says Fabulous

Fish. 'My painting is fabulous!'

Lobster likes to dance.

'My dancing is better,' says Fabulous
Fish. 'My dancing is fabulous!'

Look at me!

Octopus likes to dress up.

'My hat is better,' says Fabulous

Fish. 'My hat is fabulous!'

The other fish don't like Fabulous Fish.

Nobody wants to play with her.

'Swim with me,' says Fabulous Fish.

'No,' says Angel Fish.

'Dance with me,' says Fabulous Fish.

'No,' says Lobster.

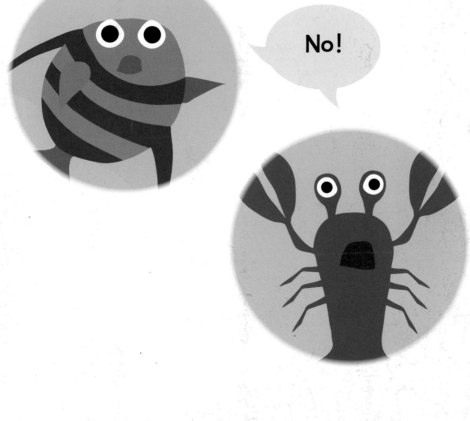

'Paint with me,' says Fabulous Fish.

'No,' says Crab.

'But I'm fabulous!' says Fabulous Fish.

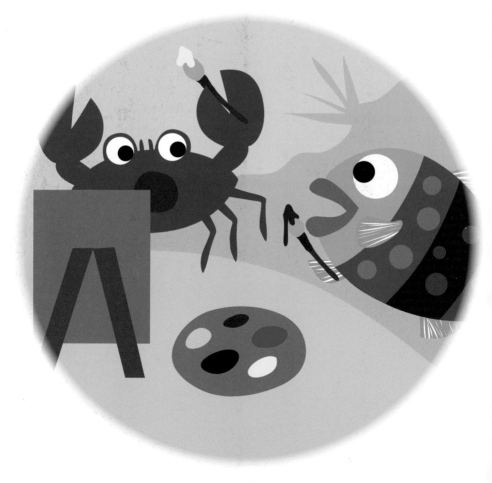

Fabulous Fish is all alone.

Fabulous Fish is sad.

'Why won't anyone be my friend?'

she says.

I don't understand.

'Because you're always boasting,'
says Seahorse.

'Because you think you're fabulous!'
says Crab.

'She IS fabulous,' says Lobster.

'But WE'RE FABULOUS TOO!'
says everyone.

'I'm sorry,' says Fabulous Fish.

Now, when Crab paints, Fabulous

Fish says, 'You're fabulous!'

When Lobster dances, Fabulous Fish

says, 'You're fabulous!'

And when they all dress up,

Fabulous Fish says,

'I love your hats! They're

FABULOUS!'